Dolphin Rescue

Adapted by Tracey West

SCHOLASTIC INC.

No part of this publication may be reproduced, stored in a retrieval system, or transmitted in any form or by any means, electronic, mechanical, photocopying, recording, or otherwise, without written permission of the publisher. For information regarding permission, write to Scholastic Inc., Attention: Permissions Department, 557 Broadway, New York, NY 10012.

ISBN 978-0-545-51655-6

LEGO, the LEGO logo and the Brick and Knob configurations are trademarks of the LEGO Group. ©2014 The LEGO Group. Produced by Scholastic Inc. under license from the LEGO Group.

Published by Scholastic Inc. SCHOLASTIC and associated logos are trademarks and/or registered trademarks of Scholastic Inc.

10 9 8 7 6 5 4 3 2 1   14 15 16 17 18 19/0

Printed in the U.S.A.   40
First printing, August 2014

Table of Contents

Chapter 1: A Science Challenge

"Yes, science class!" Andrea cheered as she and her friends walked into their classroom. "Do you know what this means?"

"Yeah, we study science," said red-haired Mia. "It's my favorite class."

"Mine, too," said Olivia. But her friends all knew that already. Olivia loved science so much that she had her own Invention Workshop.

"Rephrase," said Andrea. "It's also our last class of the day, and that means we can head for the beach after this!"

The five friends eagerly nodded. It was a bright and sunny afternoon. Hanging out at the beach after school sounded perfect!

Stephanie whipped out her smartphone. "I think I can go. Just let me check my day planner," she said. "*Ooh*, I have two free hours after school!"

Emma smiled, her green eyes shining. "I have even more than that. I'm in!"

"*Hmm*, if only there was a place for you girls to sit while I teach."

The five friends all stopped talking and turned around. Ms. Stevens, their science teacher, was at her desk looking at them through her glasses. The rest of the students were already seated and ready for class to begin.

"Oh, how about our desks?" Emma said, quickly sliding into her seat. The other girls scrambled to do the same.

Luckily, Ms. Stevens looked more amused than angry. "Wonderful idea, Emma," she said. Then she stood to begin the day's lesson. "Today we're going to be talking about dolphins."

"Dolphins . . . ocean . . . beach!" Andrea swooned with a dreamy look in her green eyes. "*Ooh*, I can feel the sand between my toes already!"

"Andrea, *shhh*!" Olivia warned.

The teacher clicked a remote in her hand, and the lights in the room dimmed. An image of a dolphin popped up on a projector screen.

"Dolphins are mammals," she began. "Some dolphins live in the ocean, and some live in rivers."

The class listened quietly as Ms. Stevens continued her lesson. She talked about where dolphins lived, what they ate, and how they communicated.

Near the end of the lesson, a photo of a fishing boat came up on the screen.

"Now I want to talk about a threat to these amazing creatures called *dolphin bycatch*," said Ms. Stevens. Another slide appeared. This one showed a fishing net in the water. Small fish were swimming into the open net—but there were dolphins swimming into it, too.

"When fishermen drag their nets through the water—or *trawl* for fish—dolphins can sometimes get caught in the net," Ms. Stevens explained.

"This is a very dangerous situation. If the dolphins can't get loose, they can drown."

She switched to another slide. It showed a dolphin tangled in the net. Without help, it couldn't get loose!

"Oh, no!" Mia gasped.

"That's awful," said Emma.

"What can they do to keep it from happening?" Stephanie asked urgently.

"That's an excellent question," Ms. Stevens said. "And one that brings us to our science contest."

She clicked her remote again, and a new picture popped up on the screen. This one was a beautiful image of a dolphin leaping happily in the ocean.

"The local fishermen are very eager to hear ideas to help them protect the dolphins. So they're offering a contest. The student—or team of students—who creates the best idea to prevent dolphin bycatch will win a dolphin sightseeing trip!"

All of the students began murmuring excitedly.

"Cool contest!"

"Awesome prize!"

Everybody wanted to win!

Just then, the bell rang. Ms. Stevens turned off the projector.

"You'll present your ideas tomorrow in class," she said. "Good luck, everyone!"

Chapter 2: Visit to the Vet

The friends all gathered around Olivia's desk as students began packing up their books. Each girl had an excited gleam in her eye. Of course, they all knew they would work together as a group.

"A dolphin sightseeing cruise would be a really fun trip," Emma said.

"*If* we win," Andrea pointed out.

Olivia shook her head. "Win or not, the important thing is that we figure out a way to help."

Andrea sighed. "I know, you're right. Still, though, it would be *awesome* if we won!"

"Okay, girls," Stephanie said, her voice taking on a confident it's-time-to-get-organized tone. "We've *sooooo* got this." Then, she realized that she didn't have any ideas. "Uh . . . *who's* got this?"

Olivia looked thoughtful. "Maybe if the nets were made out of a different material, the dolphins could slip through them."

"Cool idea, Olivia!" said Andrea.

"Dolphins also use echolocation to navigate," Mia said, remembering the lesson. "Maybe there's something there."

As the girls thought, the last student left the classroom. Emma glanced at the clock. "School's out for today."

"Yeah, but I want to stay and work on the contest," Mia said.

"Me, too," Olivia agreed.

Andrea threw up her hands. "But the beach! The sand! It's already between my toes!" She looked down at her feet. "Well, you know what I mean."

"Sorry, Andrea," Olivia said.

Stephanie smiled. "Girls, we should definitely go to the beach. Where better to get inspiration to save dolphins from bycatch?"

"Good idea," said Mia. "I just have to stop by the vet clinic to check on my animals first. Some of them are getting over injuries."

"That's okay," Emma said. "We'll all go with you. Then, we can head to the beach together afterward."

Stephanie nodded. "To the beach, then!"

They high-fived.

Olivia's Aunt Sophie ran the Heartlake Vet Clinic. All of the friends helped out there from time to time. But Mia had a special connection to the clinic—and to the animals there. She spent as much time helping Aunt Sophie as she could, and she knew every animal patient by name.

When the girls arrived, Mia headed straight to a small, brown puppy named Molly. The little pup had hurt her front right paw.

Mia gently picked Molly up and placed her on the exam table. She carefully changed the bandage. Molly tried to jump off the table, but Mia held her steady.

"Careful, Molly, that leg hasn't healed yet," she warned. She placed Molly on a soft doggie bed. The puppy wagged her tail appreciatively.

Around the room, her friends began helping the other animals. Stephanie put a carrot in a bowl and placed it in the pen of a fluffy white bunny.

Mia saw what she was doing and ran over. "Those have to be cut in pieces," she said. "Otherwise, they'll be too big for her to eat."

"Oh, okay," said Stephanie.

Meanwhile, Andrea was eagerly shaking lots of birdseed into a parrot's bowl.

"That's too much, Andrea!" Mia said, putting up a hand to stop her.

Andrea stepped aside so Mia could take out some of the birdseed. "She sure is picky," she whispered to Emma.

Emma nodded. Both girls were thinking the same thing. Lately, Mia was acting like nobody could take care of the animals as well as she could.

"It's only because she loves the animals so much," Emma whispered back. "She really worries about them!"

Just then, Aunt Sophie walked in. "Thanks so much, girls. You're doing a great job."

Aunt Sophie turned to Mia. "Now, remember, I'm out of town for the next few days. You'll be here to lend an extra hand, right?"

"Yeah. I'll be here to take care of my little guys." Mia nodded.

Then she looked around. All the animals were clean and fed. Perfect!

"Let's sweep up," Mia told her friends. "Then we can hit the road!"

Chapter 3:
Look Out!

To get to the beach, the girls drove two buggies. They zipped over the sand dunes and between palm trees before coming to a stop near the snack stand. It was the perfect beach day. The sun shone brightly in the blue sky. Turquoise waves lapped against the shore. And a gentle breeze ruffled the leaves of the palm trees.

"Woo-hoo!" the girls cheered as they unloaded a portable picnic table and chairs.

"Emma, why don't you go get us some snacks?" Stephanie suggested.

"Sure thing!" Emma agreed.

The friends quickly set up the table and chairs on the sand and sat down to start brainstorming.

"I like your idea about the nets, Olivia," Mia said. "But we should also think of how to keep the dolphins totally away from the fishermen's boats."

"Good idea," Olivia agreed. "But how?"

As they were talking, Emma returned carrying a tray of five colorful frozen drinks.

But before the friends could even reach for them, a loud beach-buggy horn blared.

They looked up and gasped. Their friend, Jacob, was driving over the sand dunes—but he was out of control! The buggy zoomed left and right, skidding wildly across the sand. Then, it careened straight toward them!

"Whoa, whoa—look out!" Jacob yelled, beeping the horn.

The friends jumped out of the way just in time. *BAM!*

Jacob crashed right into the table! The buggy tipped over into a ditch, flinging him from the driver's seat. The vehicle finally came to a stop upside down, its wheels spinning.

"Jacob!" Olivia cried. "Are you okay?"

Jacob slowly sat up, rubbing his head. "Yeah, I'm all right. A turtle was crossing the road, and I had to swerve to keep from hitting him."

"I'm just glad nobody got hurt," Mia said, breathing a sigh of relief. "Including the turtle."

"It's a good thing you honked your horn, Jacob," Stephanie said as she righted the picnic table. "It warned us just in time."

Mia put her hand on her chin. "A warning!" she said thoughtfully.

Olivia knew just what she meant. "With sound! An alarm on the nets."

Emma got it, too. "That would warn the dolphins—"

"Great idea!" Andrea interrupted, excited. "We could use underwater speakers."

"And we can call it Dolphin Alert!" suggested Stephanie.

"Perfect!" said Olivia, clasping her hands together. "Jacob, thanks for the brilliant idea!"

Jacob blushed a little. "You're welcome," he said. "What is it I did, again?"

The girls laughed. Then they got down to business. Their design for the Dolphin Alert had to be done in time for tomorrow's class!

The next day, the girls had a free period before science class. So they met up in the art room to test their project one more time.

Mia had borrowed a small fish tank from the Heartlake Pet Shop. They filled it with water. Then Olivia lowered an underwater speaker into the tank. Andrea pressed a button on her music player.

The high-pitched cry of an orca whale came out of the speaker and floated out of the water. It was perfect! Dolphins were naturally afraid of orcas. If the noise played like this next to a fishing boat's net, the dolphins wouldn't go anywhere near it!

Mia gave Olivia a thumbs-up and walked over
to Stephanie and Emma. Emma was busy drawing
on a sheet of paper with colored pencils.

"How's the poster going?" Mia asked.

"It's done!" Stephanie replied.

Emma frowned. "No, not yet," she said, rubbing
the page with her eraser.

Stephanie glanced anxiously at the clock. "Emma,
it's good enough," she insisted.

"Good enough is not . . . *good* enough!"

Emma picked up a blue pencil and started shading. Then she stopped and looked carefully at the whole poster. "I want it to be . . . *ahh* . . . perfect!"

She held up the poster so her friends could see. She had drawn a fishing boat with a Dolphin Alert speaker hanging beneath it. There were bright red sound lines coming from the speaker, and dolphins were swimming away from the lines.

"It's great!" said Mia.

Then a bell rang through the halls.

"That's the warning bell," Stephanie said. "Come on, or we'll be late!"

Chapter 4: Dolphin Alert

The friends hurried to science class, eager to share their project.

Ms. Stevens called on several students to present first, including a boy named Ben. He walked to the front of the class and propped up a poster showing an underwater traffic light. Dolphins and fish were swimming toward it from both sides.

"You can put a traffic light in the fishing area," Ben explained. "When the light turns red, the fish travel one way, and the dolphins travel the other way—away from the fisherman's nets."

"Interesting idea, Ben," said Ms. Stevens. "One question: How do the fish and dolphins know to follow the traffic lights?"

Ben shrugged. "Uh . . . traffic school?"

The class giggled, and Ben smiled sheepishly.

"Thank you, Ben," the teacher said. Then she nodded toward Mia. "Girls, it's your turn."

The friends gathered in front of the classroom. Stephanie spoke for the group. "Our idea is called Dolphin Alert. Special underwater speakers are hung from the fishing boats. When the fishermen begin to trawl with their nets, they turn on the speakers and the dolphins hear this."

She nodded toward Andrea, who pressed a button on her music player. Music streamed from the speaker.

Best friends forever,
Forever and ever . . .

"Oops! Wrong track!" Andrea said quickly.

She pressed another button, and this time, the sound of whales came through the speakers.

"Those are orcas—they are a natural enemy of dolphins," explained Olivia.

"The dolphins will swim away from the sound," said Mia.

"And they won't get caught in the nets," Emma added.

The class applauded politely as Ms. Stevens said, "Thank you, girls."

The friends walked back to their desks. Andrea rested her chin in her hand and sighed.

"And now . . . we wait to find out who the winner is."

When the final bell rang, they left school and headed to Andrea's house.

Up in her bedroom, Andrea flopped into her desk chair dramatically. "*Ugh!* A whole day to wait until we learn who won the contest!"

"Hold it together, Andrea," Mia teased.

"I don't know if I can wait until tomorrow, either!" Emma said.

"Girls, we need to find something to take our minds off the contest," Stephanie suggested.

Andrea glanced at her laptop. "I guess I could write a post on my music blog."

"And I can organize Andrea's closet!" said Stephanie, flinging open the doors.

A mountain of clothes and beach gear started to fall out, and she quickly shut the doors closed. Andrea shot her an annoyed look.

"Not that it needs organizing," Stephanie said, trying to smile.

Emma picked up a hairbrush from Andrea's dresser. "I could do someone's hair. Mia, how about you?"

Olivia grabbed her music player. "I'll play some music."

A bouncy tune started to play, and Andrea stood up.

"*Ooh*, I love this song!"

"Me, too," Emma agreed, pretending to sing into the hairbrush like it was a microphone.

I've never had a friend like you before.

You've got my back and I-I-I've got yours . . .

The girls started dancing around the room. For a while, they forgot all about the contest.

But the next morning, they each jumped out

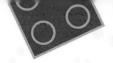

of bed, excited to find out who had won.

Mia and Olivia got to school first. They met up by the bulletin board in the main lobby where announcements were posted.

"I would love to win that dolphin trip," Mia said, scanning the board.

"Me, too!" said Olivia. But there was no sign announcing the contest winner.

Stephanie ran up to them. "Is the winner posted yet?"

Olivia shook her head. "No, not yet."

Emma ran up next. "Is the winner posted yet?"

"No," replied Mia. "And it's driving us crazy."

Andrea ran up. "Is the winner posted yet?"

"No!" the other girls said all at once.

Andrea pulled back, startled. "Whoa, what's gotten into you guys?"

Emma sighed. "Sorry, Andrea. We're just all so nervous to find out who won."

Stephanie took a deep breath. "Okay," she said. "Let's stay calm. Keep it in check. We know we did our best. If we win, great! If not, there's always next time."

Just then, Mia pointed down the hall. "Look! Ms. Stevens is coming!"

The girls all held their breath. Did the teacher have the contest results?

Chapter 5:
Getting Ready

Ms. Stevens walked up to the bulletin board, smiling. She tacked up a copy of the girls' Dolphin Alert poster . . . and then she stuck a first place ribbon on it!

"Congratulations, girls!" she told them.

"We won? We really won? Did you hear? We won!" Stephanie cheered ecstatically. She hugged her friends, and the other girls jumped up and down with excitement, too.

Ms. Stevens nodded. "Your Dolphin Alert idea was outstanding, and there are several fishing

companies interested in taking a look at it."

"Thanks, Ms. Stevens!" Mia and the others said, grinning from ear to ear. They were still so excited about winning!

"I'll see you girls on the dock tomorrow, bright and early, for the sightseeing boat trip," Ms. Stevens said. "And remember—we'll be gone all day!"

"This is going to be so much fun!" exclaimed Andrea after Ms. Stevens had left.

But Mia suddenly frowned. "Wait . . . did she say we'd be gone all day *tomorrow*? Who's going to look after my animals? Aunt Sophie won't be there!"

Emma put an arm around Mia. "Don't worry, Mia. I'm sure we can find someone at the clinic who can fill in. We'll check after school."

Mia nodded. But she looked a little doubtful.

After school, Mia and Emma headed straight for the Heartlake Vet Clinic. When they arrived, they found an assistant named Ashley at the front desk. Ashley worked full-time for Olivia's Aunt Sophie.

"Hi, Ashley," Mia said. "I need a favor . . ."

Mia explained how she had promised to work on Saturday, but that was before she knew she and her friends had won the contest.

"Sorry, Mia. I'm going away this weekend, too," Ashley said. "But Sasha might be free. Why don't you ask her?" She nodded toward a dark-haired woman across the room.

As Ashley walked away, Mia turned to Emma and groaned. "Now I *really* can't go!"

Emma was confused. "What about Sasha? We haven't checked with her yet."

Mia frowned. "Sasha's nice and everything, but she just started here, and—"

The sound of a yapping puppy interrupted her. Sasha was about to put a kitten in the same cage as the dog, and both animals were frightened!

"Oops, wrong cage!" Sasha laughed nervously, quickly removing the kitten.

"See what I mean?" Mia said quietly to Emma. "You want me to trust *her*?"

"Sophie does," Emma reminded her. "And maybe you can show Sasha how you like things done."

Mia sighed. "Okay. Let's go ask her."

Mia walked over to Sasha, who was about to change the bandage on Molly, the brown puppy.

"Hi, Sasha," Mia said.

Sasha looked up and smiled. "Hi, Mia."

"So, I was wondering if you could work for me tomorrow?" Mia asked tentatively. "I promised Sophie I'd be here, but my friends and I won this contest, and we're supposed to go on a dolphin sightseeing trip tomorrow."

"That sounds amazing!" said Sasha. "No problem. I'm happy to fill in."

"Thanks," Mia said. But she still sounded doubtful. She watched as Sasha picked up Molly and wrapped a new bandage around her paw.

"She likes the bandage looser than that!" Mia insisted.

"Oh, sorry, girl!" Sasha told Molly. She unwound the bandage and started again.

"Slower!" Mia instructed.

Emma tapped Mia on the shoulder. "Mia, would you come here a sec?" she asked, gently leading her away. "I think you're making Sasha nervous hovering over her like that."

"Me, making *her* nervous?" Mia asked.

"Sasha isn't you," Emma pointed out. "She's going to have her own way of doing things."

"You mean the wrong way," Mia said. "I don't know, Emma. Maybe it's best if I just skip the sightseeing trip."

At that moment, Mia heard Molly give a happy bark. She turned around. The puppy's bandage was wrapped perfectly! She cuddled in Sasha's arms, happily nuzzling her face.

"Wow, Sasha!" Mia said, walking over. "You did a great job. Molly looks so happy!"

Sasha smiled appreciatively. "Thanks, Mia.

That means a lot. I think I'm getting the hang of things here."

Mia looked at Emma and grinned. "I think you're right. My little guys will be in good hands with Sasha. I'm going on the trip!"

Chapter 6:
All Aboard

Early the next morning, Stephanie, Andrea, Mia, Emma, and Olivia got to the dock. Each wore a long yellow rain slicker and rubber boots.

"Oh, that must be our boat," Stephanie guessed, pointing to a small green fishing boat.

"Morning, girls!"

The friends turned around at the sound of their science teacher's cheerful voice. When they saw her, they were surprised. Ms. Stevens looked super fashionable, with a purple tank top, white wraparound skirt, and sunglasses.

Emma grinned. "Looks like Ms. Stevens is going to be the best dressed on the boat."

"Oh, that's not our boat, girls," said Ms. Stevens. "*That's* our boat."

She pointed to a gleaming white yacht docked a little farther down. The three-story yacht had a colorful party deck and a slide that went from the second floor to the main level.

"A yacht?" Stephanie asked in disbelief.

"No way!" Olivia cried.

"Seriously?" asked Mia.

"I—I don't even have words for how cool this is!" Andrea swooned.

"I do," said Emma. "Sweet ride!"

Ms. Stevens grinned. "Did I forget to mention this part?"

The girls nodded.

"Uh, yeah!" said Mia.

Just then, a boy walked off the yacht to meet them. He had blond hair, blue eyes, and wore a light blue shirt with a sailboat on the pocket.

Ms. Stevens waved at him. "Hi, Andrew!"

Andrew waved back. "Hi!"

The girls looked up at the fancy yacht. Then they looked down at their raincoats and boots.

"Ms. Stevens, this is just not right!" Andrea protested.

Ms. Stevens raised an eyebrow, surprised. "What do you mean?"

"We can't take a *yacht* looking like this!" Andrea and the girls pointed to their wet-weather gear.

"Please, Ms. Stevens," Stephanie begged. "Can we go home quickly and change? We'll be back in fifteen minutes, promise!"

"All right, girls, but hurry," the teacher said.

The girls raced off the dock. Fifteen minutes later, they came back just like they had promised. But this time, they were definitely dressed for a yacht cruise! Emma, Andrea, and Mia all wore bright beach shorts while Olivia and Stephanie sported

pretty waist wraps. Each had a colorful bathing suit top and matching sunglasses.

"Now, *this* is what I'm talking about!" said Stephanie.

"Come on aboard!" Andrew called out. "Watch your step."

As the girls boarded, Emma looked through her bag. "I forgot my camera in the car. Be right back!" She dashed off.

Her friends began to explore the yacht. On the first floor they found a cute little bedroom tucked away. Next to it was a full kitchen. There was even a living room with a huge, comfy couch.

"Look at the seating!" Andrea said, flopping onto the couch.

Next, they made their way to the top deck, where Andrew was steering the yacht. From there they could see the ocean stretch out before them. It sparkled in the morning sunlight.

"Amazing view!" Mia said.

Then they went back down to the first level. At the end of the boat was a sun deck with lounge chairs. The girls put on sunscreen and relaxed.

"I could spend some serious time here," Andrea remarked.

"It's official: This yacht is kickin'," said Stephanie.

"Totally," agreed Mia. "Emma, you're awfully quiet. What do you think?"

There was no answer.

"Emma?" Mia asked again. By now all the girls

were looking around the deck. Where was Emma?

Suddenly, Mia's phone buzzed, and she picked it up. "It's Emma, you guys," she said. "Hello?"

"You left me on the dock!" Emma's voice shouted through the phone speaker.

The girls looked at one another in shock. They couldn't believe they'd left their friend!

Mia and Olivia raced below deck and found Ms. Stevens in the living room.

"We forgot Emma!" Mia cried.

"She's still on the dock!" added Olivia.

"Oh, dear," said Ms. Stevens. "What should we do?"

Stephanie and Andrea joined them.

"We're not that far out," said Stephanie. "We could turn around."

"Yeah, turn around," repeated Andrea.

"Right, like I just said," Stephanie replied.

"No," said Andrea. "I mean, *turn around*!" She pointed off the deck of the boat behind them to a Wet-Ski attached to the yacht.

"A Wet-Ski! One of us could get Emma!" Mia said.

"I will!" Olivia raced to the edge of the deck.

But Mia, Andrea, and Stephanie jumped in front of her.

"No, I will!" said Mia.

"No, me!" said Stephanie.

"I saw it first!" Andrea pointed out.

While the girls bantered, Olivia tiptoed behind them. She slipped on a life jacket. Then she climbed up to the top of the slide. She slid down—and landed right on the Wet-Ski!

"Be back soon!" Olivia called out with a wave.

Mia shook her head. "She's fast."

"And sneaky," Andrea added.

Olivia zipped across the water and quickly got back to the dock. She stopped the Wet-Ski right next to Emma.

"Sorry!" she called.

"It's okay," Emma said. "Let's go!"

When they got back to the yacht, the girls spent the rest of the morning enjoying being out on the ocean. They played music, relaxed on deck, and ate a delicious lunch. It was perfect—except they hadn't seen any dolphins yet.

Emma stretched out on a lounge chair to catch some sun. "This is so great!" she said.

"I just hope we see some dolphins before the day is over," Stephanie said.

As if on cue, Mia called down from the upper deck. "Look, you guys! Dolphins!"

Everyone got up and ran to the rails to look. Not too far away, a pod of dolphins was leaping over the waves. The smooth, gray creatures made happy noises as they swam.

"Wow," said Olivia. "I've never been this close to dolphins before."

"Me neither," said Andrea. "They're beautiful!"

Olivia smiled as she watched the happy creatures playing in the waves. She looked left . . . and suddenly, her face fell. "Oh, no. Fishing boats!"

She pointed into the distance where two fishing boats were lowering nets into the water.

"And their trawling nets are out!" Mia realized. "This is terrible. The fishermen must not see the dolphins. If we don't do something, the dolphins will get trapped!"

Chapter 7:
To the Rescue!

The friends all looked at one another. What could they do to protect the dolphins from the fishermen's nets?

"I brought our Dolphin Alert system," Andrea suddenly realized. "Maybe we can try it!"

The girls moved quickly. They asked Andrew to steer the yacht as close to the fishing boats as possible. Stephanie hooked up the under water speaker to a music player.

Andrew maneuvered them into a spot between the dolphin pod and the boats. The dolphins were swimming closer and closer to the nets. There wasn't a minute to waste!

"Okay, it's ready," Stephanie said, and she dropped the Dolphin Alert speaker into the water.

"Dolphin Alert, do your thing!" Andrea cried.

The orca whale sounds echoed through the water. But the dolphins were still swimming toward the nets. The girls held their breaths.

Would their invention work?

Then, at the last second, the dolphins heard the warning! They turned around just before they reached the nets. From the top deck, Olivia had a clear view of the creatures as they swam away from the boats.

"It's working!" Olivia cried. "The dolphins are changing course!"

The friends let out a cheer. A fisherman on the nearest boat smiled and waved.

"Good work, girls," he told them.

The five friends were so happy. Not only had they seen the dolphins, but they had helped protect them, too. This was turning out to be an incredible sightseeing trip!

Now that the dolphins were safe, Andrew started up the yacht engine again to head home.

The friends chatted about the incredible day as their yacht pulled away from the fishing boats. Suddenly, Mia spotted something in the water off the stern. She walked to the edge, peered down, and gasped.

"Oh, no. Andrew, stop!" she yelled up to the top deck.

"What's going on?" Andrew asked.

"There's a baby dolphin who got separated from the group!" Mia called out.

The friends ran over and saw that Mia was right. Down in the water, a little baby dolphin was all alone. And he looked frightened.

"We have to help him find his family!" said Andrea.

Olivia ran to grab a pair of binoculars. "I'll look for the pod," she said, scanning the ocean.

As her friend searched for the group of

dolphins, Emma leaned over the deck and put out a hand for the baby dolphin. Curious, he swam up to her.

"Don't worry, little guy," she said, gently patting him on the head. "We've got you."

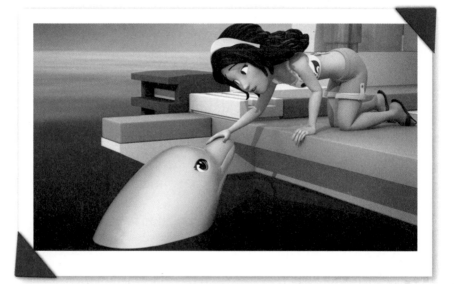

Finally, Olivia spotted the dolphin pod in the distance. "There! Starboard side, Andrew!"

Andrew started to turn the ship to the right. "Is he following us?" he called down.

"Yes!" Stephanie replied.

But then, she noticed something. The baby dolphin was following closely—too closely. He was just feet away from the yacht's whirling propeller!

"Stop the engine! The propeller will hurt him!" Stephanie yelled up.

Andrew stopped the engine. Exasperated, the girls looked at one another. If they couldn't pilot the ship, how would they get the baby dolphin back to his family?

With a sudden burst of excitement, Andrea clapped her hands. "I know what to do," she cried.

With that, Andrea dove into the water! She quickly swam toward the baby dolphin and held out a hand to show she was friendly. The dolphin came closer, and she patted his nose.

Then Andrea swam up to the surface. Her idea was working—the baby dolphin followed her! She put her arm around his back and kicked her feet to direct him toward the pod.

As Andrea and the baby dolphin drew near,
the pod realized it was missing one of their own.
Quickly, they swam back to meet Andrea and the
baby. One dolphin swam ahead of the group, and
the baby chirped happily and swam toward her.

"That must be the baby's mom," Mia guessed
from where she and the others were watching
aboard the yacht.

Andrea smiled as the baby nuzzled his mother's
cheek. Then another dolphin swam up and
stopped next to Andrea. It made a noise, and
Andrea understood. She put her arm around it, and

the dolphin gracefully glided back to the yacht.

Andrea climbed off the dolphin and back on deck. She was trembling with excitement!

Stephanie kneeled down and patted the dolphin's head. The dolphin was making happy chirping noises.

"I don't speak dolphin, but I think she's thanking us," she said.

The friends laughed. "That makes me think of my animals," Mia said. "I hope they're okay."

"Why don't you call Sasha?" Emma suggested.

"Great idea," Mia said, taking out her phone. But her excitement was short lived. "Oh, no. There's no signal. I guess we're too far out at sea."

"Don't worry," Emma said. "I'm sure they're fine. We're heading back now anyway. You can text her in a little bit."

Andrew turned the engine back on, and the yacht slowly drifted away from the dolphin pod. The girls waved as the dolphins swam away.

"Bye! Don't lose each other!" Andrea called.

"Be careful!" added Mia.

By this time, the rays of the setting sun were streaking the sky with orange. Olivia admired the beautiful sunset from the top deck. She was about to comment on it to her friends when, without warning, she heard a loud beep coming from behind her.

It was Andrew's navigation system. It beeped several more times, then the screen went blank.

"Oh, great," Andrew said with a sigh. "The GPS is out."

"Maybe I can help," Olivia offered.

"It's linked to that computer," Andrew said, pointing to a nearby laptop.

Olivia started typing on the laptop. Ms. Stevens noticed that the yacht had stopped moving again and called up to the deck.

"Is there a problem, Andrew?"

"We lost our navigation system, but Olivia's trying to fix it," Andrew replied.

Olivia looked at the screen. She was just typing in another command when the computer screen went blank, too! "Uhh, we might want to have a Plan B," she said.

"You're telling me," Andrew said. "Without GPS, we have no way of knowing where we are."

Soon it would be dark. If they couldn't get the GPS back up soon, they could be lost all night!

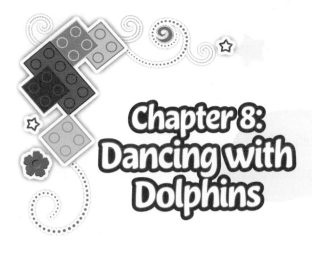

Chapter 8: Dancing with Dolphins

Ms. Stevens stayed calm. "Quite a challenge," she said. She turned to Andrea and her friends. "What do you girls think we should do?"

"Well, we can't use our cell phones," Mia pointed out.

"We could send a Mayday signal to the Coast Guard," Andrea suggested.

Ms. Stevens nodded. "Yes, that's one solution."

Stephanie looked thoughtful. "We know we traveled northeast to get here, right?"

"Yeah," Andrea agreed.

"That means we need to go southwest to get back to the dock," Stephanie said.

"We can figure out southwest, like sailors used to," Emma said. "They didn't have GPS."

Mia looked out over the ocean. "I know! We can use the sun as a compass point. It sets in the west."

"And it's starting to set now," Andrea said, pointing. The girls got up and walked to the yacht's rail. The sun was sinking low on the horizon.

"If that's west, then southwest should be that way," Mia said, pointing.

Emma looked. "Yeah, out by the dolphins. I think the dolphins are pointing the way home!"

She was right. In the distance, the dolphin pod eagerly jumped and splashed in the water, heading southwest.

"It's their ocean," Andrea exclaimed happily. "They would know!"

Andrew steered the yacht toward the dolphins. Meanwhile, Olivia had not given up on the GPS. Adjusting some of the computer's wires, she rebooted the system.

"Try the GPS now," she told Andrew.

He flipped the switch back on . . . and the screen lit up, showing the direction in which they were going!

"Southwest!" Olivia said. "We were right!"

Ms. Stevens smiled. "Good work, everyone!"

Now that they were heading back within

cell-phone range, Mia's smartphone suddenly beeped. Sasha had sent her a photo of Molly and the kitten. Both of the pets looked happy as could be, nuzzling and licking Sasha's face.

"Look! My little guys are doing great," Mia said with a grin.

"I think this calls for celebration music," Andrea declared. She plugged her music player into the yacht's sound system. A bouncy tune came from the speakers.

The summer is on, we're hanging out.
Such a pretty day to take a ride.
We have so much fun, just playing 'round
You always find a way to make me smile.
We're like the perfect team.
We're looking out for each other!
Everywhere we go,
We stick together.
Cruising with the girls,
Friends are forever!

Some of the dolphins swam closer. They slapped their tails on the water to the beat of the music. The girls danced on the deck, and as they did, the dolphins began jumping and twirling in the water, too.

"Look! They want to dance with us!" said Stephanie.

The friends continued to rock out on the deck while the dolphins danced in the water. Emma, Mia, Stephanie, Olivia, and Andrea all smiled.

Today had been the perfect day. They'd been on a fabulous cruise, they'd seen dolphins, and they'd even rescued the dolphins from danger.

But best of all, they had done it together. As the yacht sailed home over the sparkling water, the friends knew Andrea's song was right.

Nothing was better than being together!